With thanks to Mom and Dad for the inspiration, Eva for the means, and Aunt Jo for the bookbinding kit (and so much more) —A. M. B.

For Des, Ed, and Sean, and for their families —L. D.

flying feet

a story of irish dance

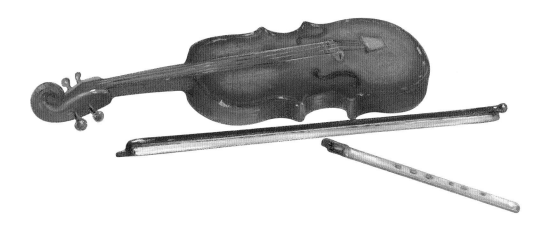

By Anna Marlis Burgard

Illustrated by Leighanne Dees

chronicle books · san francisco

The wind raced across the sea like a great herd of stallions,
leaping over islands and kicking up waves on the way to the small cottage in
Ballyconneely where Gabriel Feeney lay sleeping. As the rattling of the windows
shook the boy awake, two strangers rode toward his village.

Aidan Delaney rode his galloping mare with the wind at his back, whipping his wild hair and woolen cloak all about.

Michael MacHugh, with his slick hair and fancy tweed suit, furiously pedaled his bicycle against the gusts.

The men were quite different in spirit, but they had two things in common: both were grand dancers, and both were determined to teach their steps to every able body in Ballyconneely.

When Gabriel heard the clip-clop of the horse's hooves, he ran outside, calling, "*Dia daoibh!*—Hello! What brings you to Ballyconneely?"

Michael and Aidan both replied, "I've come to teach the dancing."

The strangers stared at each other in disbelief, scarcely trusting their own ears. How could it be that they arrived at exactly the *same* moment, in the *same* village, hoping for the *same* work?

Michael edged up close to Aidan and narrowed his eyes. "Now, lad, what makes you think you and your shoddy boots could teach anyone to dance? I am Michael MacHugh, champion of all County Galway. I shall teach the good people of Ballyconneely to dance."

Aidan stood tall and stared back at Michael. "The boots may be old and worn, but the feet inside them are young and swift. I am Aidan Delaney, and I've not lost a competition in *any* county of Ireland."

When Gabriel's father, Brendan, heard the arguing, he came outside and said, "There's only one way to settle this. Gabriel, fetch the fiddle and whistle. Gentlemen, shake hands, and may the better man win."

The men lifted the Feeney's half door from its creaking hinges and placed it in the road.

They drew straws to see who would be first to dance. Michael pulled the longer straw.

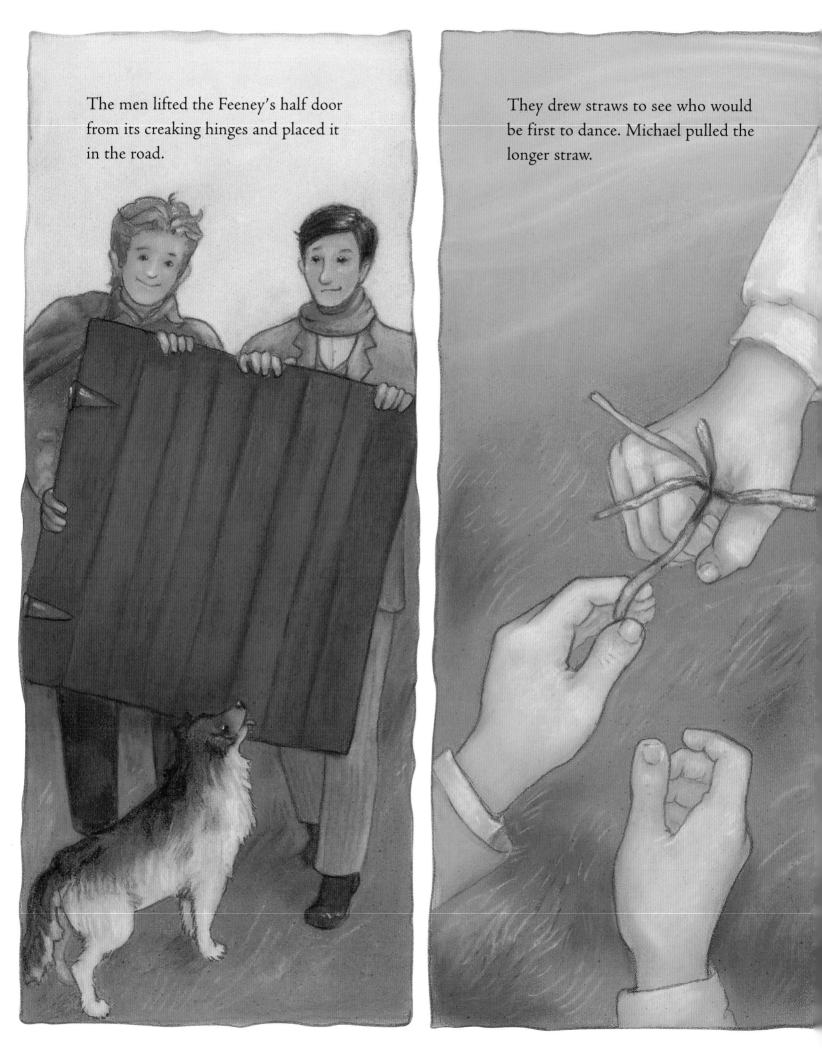

He took off his jacket, and set to clearing the dust from the door. Brendan bowed up as Gabriel blew *dum-diddle dees* into the breeze. Aidan chose a tune that would put his opponent's skill to the test.

"Let's see how your feet keep time with 'The Blue-eyed Rascal,'" he said.

"Watch and learn," said Michael, stepping onto the door.

With the very first zings from the strings, Michael shot straight into the air, as light and quick as an arrow. He landed with a mighty thundering of feet, striking the wood with his soles as if kicking stones aside, crossing left over right, right over left.

He didn't miss a single beat, and as the tune wound down, he bounded from corner to corner of the door, finishing right in front of Aidan, who shouted, "Nicely done!"

The audience grew as the music drew the neighbors near. Michael asked Aidan, "Could you step about to a hornpipe? Perhaps 'The Rambling Rake'?"

"With pleasure," Aidan said, tossing off his cloak.

Brendan slid his bow across the strings as Gabriel blew into the whistle. Aidan tapped his foot in time, then with a loud shout leapt as high as the hedgerow. He flicked his feet out in front of him and battered the boards as he landed, sending clouds of dust flying. Everyone cheered for his powerful dancing—and wondered how Michael would best him.

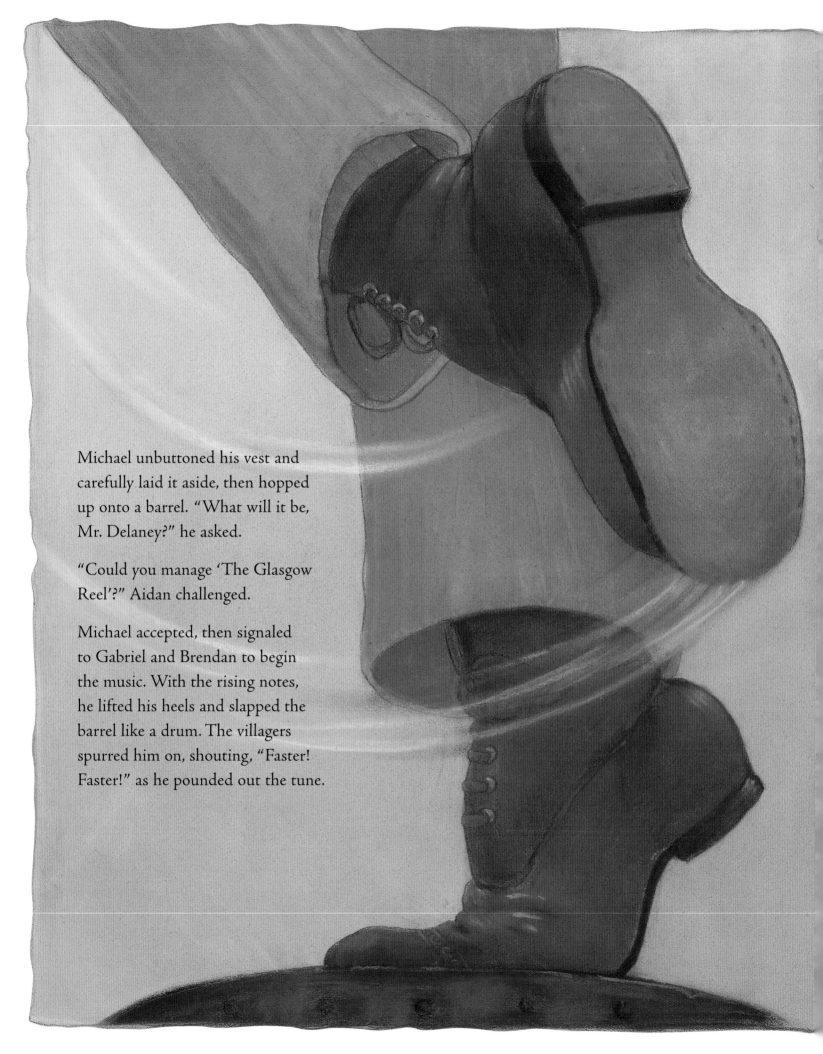

Michael unbuttoned his vest and carefully laid it aside, then hopped up onto a barrel. "What will it be, Mr. Delaney?" he asked.

"Could you manage 'The Glasgow Reel'?" Aidan challenged.

Michael accepted, then signaled to Gabriel and Brendan to begin the music. With the rising notes, he lifted his heels and slapped the barrel like a drum. The villagers spurred him on, shouting, "Faster! Faster!" as he pounded out the tune.

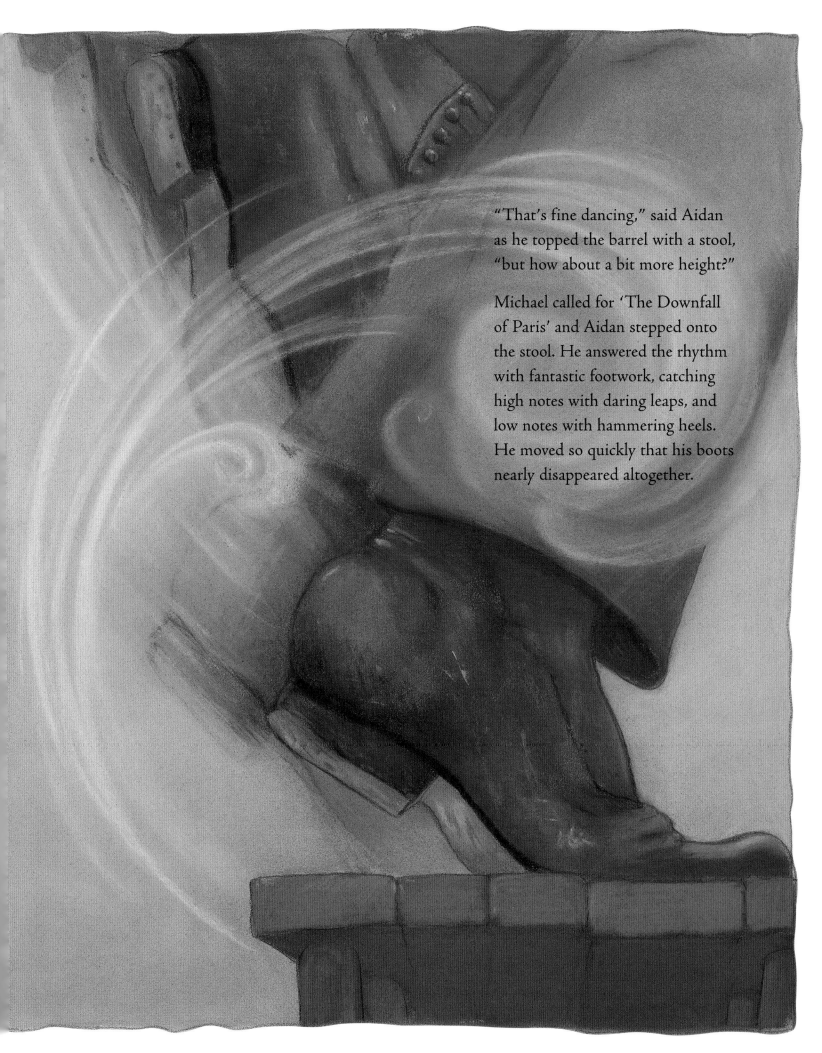

"That's fine dancing," said Aidan as he topped the barrel with a stool, "but how about a bit more height?"

Michael called for 'The Downfall of Paris' and Aidan stepped onto the stool. He answered the rhythm with fantastic footwork, catching high notes with daring leaps, and low notes with hammering heels. He moved so quickly that his boots nearly disappeared altogether.

Michael scowled as the crowd cheered for Aidan, but only for a moment. He rolled up his sleeves and sprang onto an old stone wall. Aidan called out, "Why don't you try 'The Kilkenny Races' on that track of stones?" The crowd gasped—could the man keep his balance on that narrow surface to such a fast-paced tune as that?

But Michael MacHugh was fueled by faith. He danced with such lightning speed—high in the air, firm on the stones, cutting back and across—that he landed his final steps in silence as everyone stared, wide-eyed and wonder filled.

Michael was confident that the competition was his.

The villagers gathered around Michael
to praise his performance. Gabriel knew
he'd danced brilliantly, but his heart
went out to Aidan. How could he hope
to win now? He turned to comfort him,
but Aidan was nowhere to be seen.

Then Gabriel spotted Aidan climbing up to the roof. The boy ran toward him shouting, "What can you be doing? *Bi curamach*—Be careful! You'll fall to your death!"

Aidan laughed and said, "Don't worry yourself, lad. Just tell the others to come around. This contest isn't finished yet!"

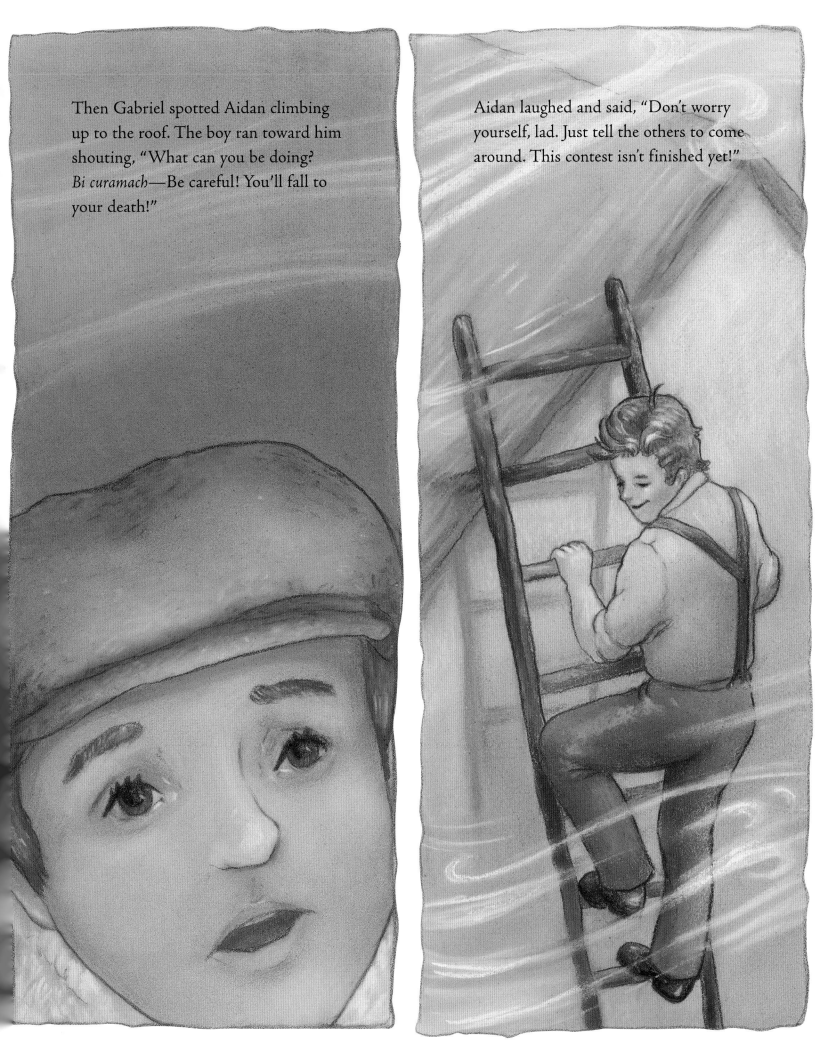

Michael could not believe his eyes—Aidan was climbing onto the chimney. "Well, if he's going to risk life and limb, I'll pick the perfect melody to match his foolishness." He considered all the reels he knew. Then it came to him, a tune that only the very best master could keep time with. "Would you favor us with 'The Cooley Races,' Mr. Delaney?" he shouted up. Aidan accepted his challenge with a mischievous grin and then. . .

...*s w o o s h!* Up into the air he flew!
First a scissor kick!
Then back double clicks!
Then a salmon's leap!

He sprang into the heavens, performing
every known step—and creating one
after another that not a soul had seen
the likes of.

Joyful cheers filled Aidan's ears as he stepped to the final notes. He hopped off the chimney and slid down the thatch, knowing that he had danced his very best. Gentlemen stepped forward to offer congratulations. Ladies waited to be introduced. And though Michael MacHugh was not a man who liked to lose, he had to admit that he, too, had been spellbound.

Brendan shook Aidan's hand and said, "*Cead mile failte*—one hundred thousand welcomes." And with those words, Aidan Delaney became the dancing master of Ballyconneely.

That evening, all of Ballyconneely gathered for a bonfire dance. Aidan and Michael took turns dancing with the ladies until the wind lifted the last sparks from the embers far out to sea.

Gabriel listened as the storytellers began weaving bits of magic into what they had all seen with their own mortal eyes:

"*Ababúna*—good heavens! Didn't he float there above the cottage as if the very wind held him?" whispered Mrs. Tierney.

"'Twas as though he had wings!" Gabriel agreed.

"Aye, he was like an angel upon the clouds," declared Mr. O'Flaherty.

It was no time at all before the contest was transformed into legend. Yet no matter how many facts faded with each new telling, this truth remained: never before, and never since, had any living body in Ballyconneely witnessed the likes of Aidan Delaney and his flying feet.

A NOTE ABOUT IRISH DANCE

For the good are always the merry,
Save by an evil chance,
And the merry love the fiddle
And the merry love to dance:

And when the folk there spy me,
They will all come up to me,
With 'Here is the fiddler of Dooney!'
And dance like a wave of the sea.

from "The Fiddler of Dooney" by William Butler Yeats

Dancing is a festive part of Irish life—a living art form that's survived invasions, famines, and emigrations. Druids danced as they worshiped the sun and trees, and ever since those ancient times (and perhaps before) the Irish have kicked up their heels not only to celebrate important occasions, but also to bring cheer to ordinary days. They've danced indoors on hearthstones and kitchen tables, and outdoors on the packed earth of dirt crossroads and doors taken off their hinges. They dance to this day to the music of fiddles, flutes, and bagpipes, and when no instruments are available, to singing or clapping or whistling. They have danced defiantly when English overlords and their own priests forbade it.

Dancing is for rich and poor alike, so there's always been a steady demand for masters. In centuries past, these itinerant men, and a few women, traveled around the countryside offering instruction in exchange for wages and a place to stay. A village could support only one master, so if by chance two arrived at the same time, they'd agree to test each other's talents against a variety of reels and hornpipes. One contestant would name a familiar tune, then his opponent would try to match his footwork to keep time with the tempo. In a competition called "dancing the heights," they would perform on higher and higher, smaller and smaller surfaces until one of them couldn't keep up with the music, or couldn't dance any higher off the ground.

During the nineteenth century, when so many Irish left their homeland, many of these dances traveled the globe. More recently, stage productions such as *Celtic Thunder* and *Riverdance* have made the beauty of Irish step dancing even more famous. The tradition of Irish dance is alive and well in hundreds of homes, schools, and churches from Ireland to America to Australia, and in competitions which continue to test the skills of the men, women, and children who inspire each other to perform their best.

Acknowledgments

A host of generous professionals helped guide *Flying Feet* to the finish: Evelyn Coleman, Bob Frigo, Felice Holman, Marc Nadel, Gwen Strauss, and Jo Trueschler all read versions of the text and offered valuable feedback. Champion step dancer and instructor Abbey Pride reviewed the dancers' stances, and assisted with selecting the vareties of dances and names of the tunes to ensure that the escalation in difficulty was accurate. Stefanie Stronge and Lisa Cregan-O'Brien lent us their Irish ears to make sure the words rang true. David Dirlam of The Folk Traditions Store in Savannah verified the musicians' positions, and listened for the way the music was described.

At Chronicle Books, Victoria Rock, Sara Gillingham, and Beth Weber shepherded our words with sterling sensibilities, and kindness. Whenever they asked for more, or less, it was a step in the right direction.

The Irish musicians and dancers who perfected their art forms, and carried on these traditions through the centuries, inspired this story. We thank them for their spirit and dedication.

—A. M. B. and L. D.

Pronunciation Guide for Gaelic Words

Gaelic—or Irish as it's known by those who speak it—is one of several Celtic languages that were once widely spoken across Western and Northern Europe. Although Ireland was a Gaelic-speaking country until the 16th century, and while the Republic of Ireland is bilingual (English and Irish), and Northern Ireland is trilingual (English, Irish, and Ulster Scots), only about 10 percent of the native Irish speak the language fluently.

As with many languages, the pronunciations of Irish can vary from city to town and from home to home; still, the pronunciations below are an accurate introduction to the way the words sound.

Dia daoibh [DYEE-uh deev] = Hello (literally, "God to you"—addressing more than one person)
Bi curamach [BEE KOO-ruh-mukh] = Be careful
Cead mile failte [KAYD MEE-luh FAWL-tyuh] = One hundred thousand welcomes
Ababúna [AH-buh-BOON-uh] = Good heavens

Selected Bibliography

Boullier, Diann. *Exploring Irish Music and Dance*. Dublin: O'Brien Press, 1998.

Brennan, Helen. *The Story of Irish Dance*. Belfast: Roberts Rinehart Publishers, 2001.

Cullinane, Dr. John. *Aspects of the History of Irish Ceili Dancing 1897-1997*. Cork City: Dr. John Cullinan, 1998.

Flynn, Arthur. *Irish Dance*. Gretna: Pelican Publishing Company, 1998.

Smyth, Sam. *Riverdance: The Story*. London: Andre Duetsch, 1996.

Whelan, Frank. *The Complete Guide to Irish Dance*. Belfast: Appletree Press, 2000.

Design by Anna Marlis Burgard and Angela Rojas.
Title type design by Janice Shay.
The text type was set in Adobe Jenson and Stone Serif.
The illustrations were created with Nupastel and Rembrandt pastels, Conte pastel pencils, and Prismacolor
pencils on Sennelier La Carte Pastel Card.
Produced by Design Press, a division of the Savannah College of Art and Design.
www.designpressbooks.com

Manufactured in China.

Library of Congress Cataloging-in-Publication Data
Burgard, Anna Marlis.
Flying feet : a story of Irish dance / by Anna Marlis Burgard ; illustrated by Leighanne Dees.
p. cm.
Summary: Based on a true tale, two master dancers compete for the chance to teach
the people of Ballyconneely, Ireland, how to dance.
ISBN 0-8118-4431-5
[1. Dance—Fiction. 2. Contests—Fiction. 3. Ireland—Fiction.] I. Dees, Leighanne, ill. II. Title.
PZ7.B91628Fl 2005
[Fic]—dc22
2004008485

Distributed in Canada by Raincoast Books
9050 Shaughnessy Street, Vancouver, British Columbia V6P 6E5

10 9 8 7 6 5 4 3 2 1

Chronicle Books LLC
85 Second Street, San Francisco, California 94105

www.chroniclekids.com

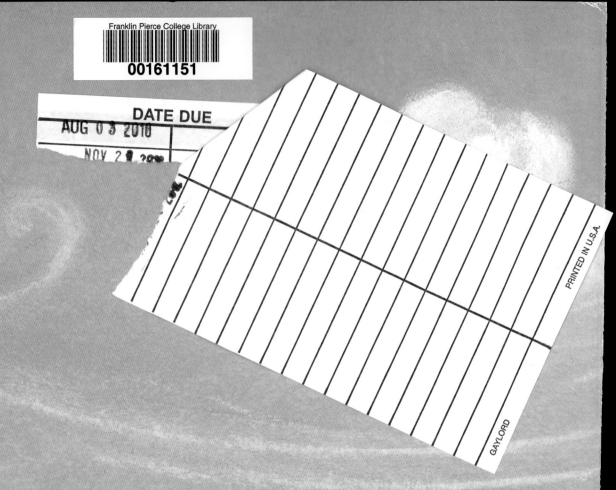